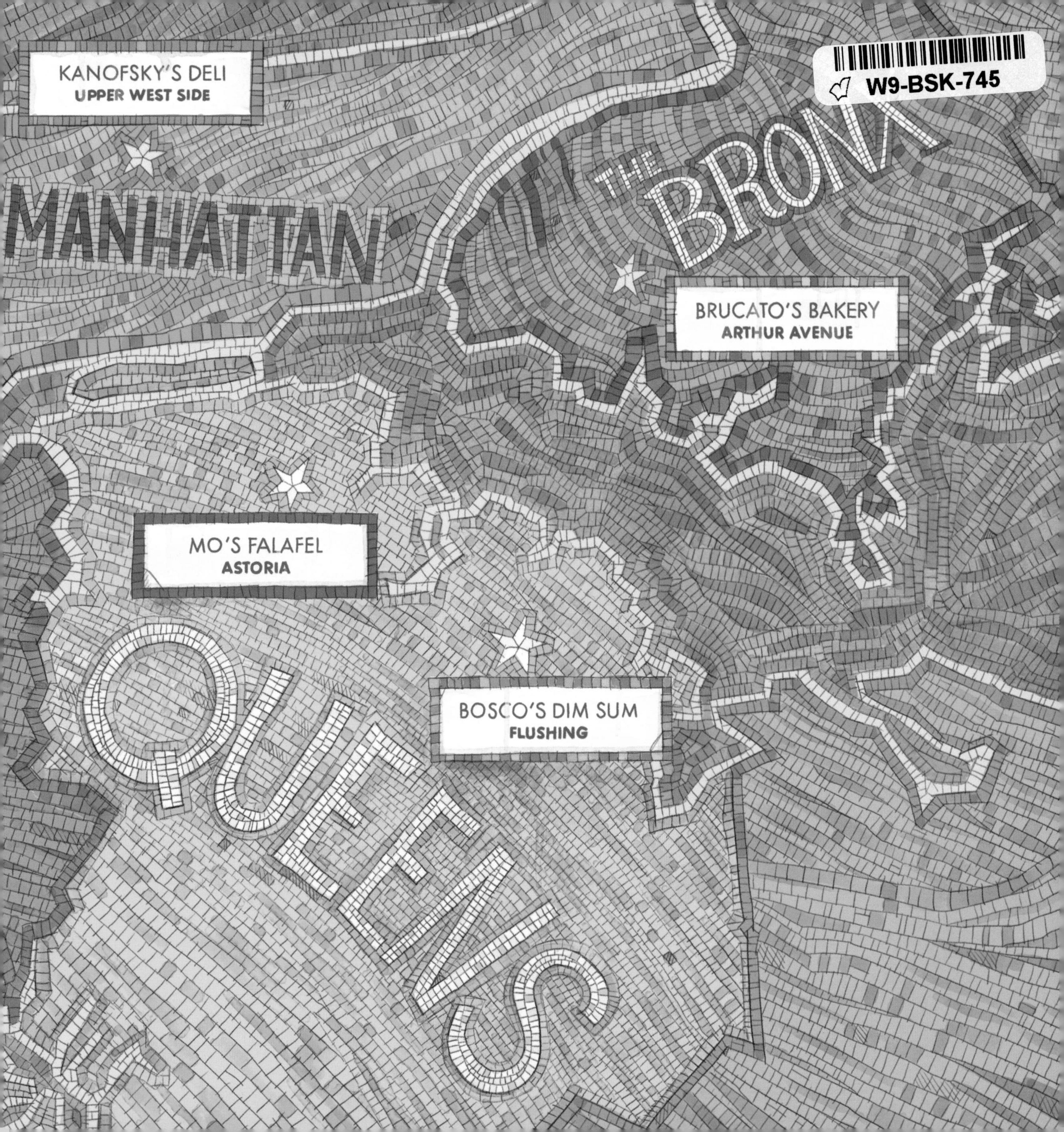
KANOFSKY'S DELI
UPPER WEST SIDE
MANHATTAN
THE BRONX
BRUCATO'S BAKERY
ARTHUR AVENUE
MO'S FALAFEL
ASTORIA
QUEENS
BOSCO'S DIM SUM
FLUSHING

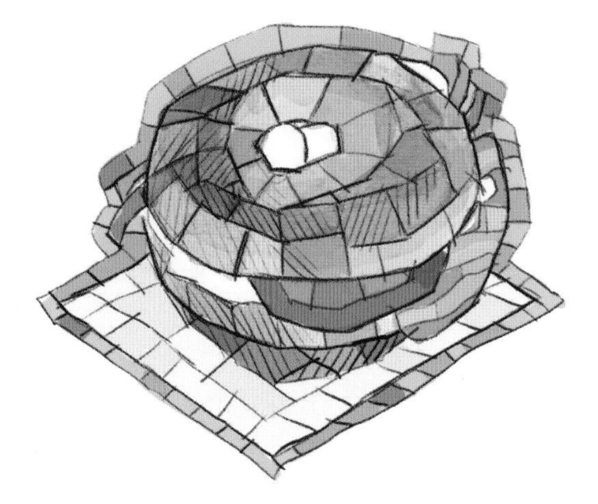

For Lucy, Jon, Maggie, and Drew, in honor of a bagel brunch so incredible, you dedicate a book in its memory years later.

ARCHAIA™

tudios, 5670 Wilshire Boulevard, Suite 400, Los Angeles, CA 90036-5679.

China. First Printing.

-1-68415-424-1, eISBN: 978-1-64144-541-2

BOLIVAR™
EATS NEW YORK
A DISCOVERY ADVENTURE™

SEAN RUBIN

Published by
ARCHAIA™
Los Angeles, California

Kanofsky's
DELICATESSEN
RESTAURANT
SANDWICHES • SOUP • KNISHES • SODA
YOU ORDERED A CORNED BEEF SANDWICH...AGAIN?
SO WHAT?
IT'S ALL YOU EAT! DON'T YOU LIKE ANY OTHER FOOD?
...NO.

PASTRAMI
SALAMI
CORNED BEEF
CHOPPED LIVER
TURKEY
BOLOGNA
ROAST BEEF
LIVERWURST
SQUARE KNISH
KASHA VARNISHKS
LATKES
MATZOH BALLS
WAIT. HAVE YOU EVEN **TRIED** ANY OTHER KINDS OF FOOD?
NO.
HOW DO YOU KNOW YOU DON'T LIKE SOMETHING IF YOU HAVEN'T TRIED IT?
DINOSAURS ARE INSIGHTFUL LIKE THAT.
ORDER NUMBER 15-
UH... DOUBLE-DELUXE CORNED BEEF...
TO GO!
THANKS!
HEY!!
LISTEN- IF YOU WANT THIS SANDWICH, I'LL MAKE YOU A DEAL.
BUT...

I ALREADY PAID FOR IT...
COME WITH ME AND TRY SOME DIFFERENT FOOD...
IF YOU EAT EVERYTHING...
I'LL GIVE YOU THIS SANDWICH!
BUT IT'S ALREADY MY SANDWICH.
SIGH.
FINE.

WHERE ARE WE GOING, ANYWAY?
I HAVE A FEW IDEAS...
OBAGE
BEST IN N.Y.C.

Kanofsky's Deli

Manhattan — Upper West Side

Every day, Bolivar orders at least one corned beef sandwich at Kanofsky's, his neighborhood kosher deli. Kosher delis follow *kashrut*, a set of rules that some Jewish people use for preparing food and for knowing what kind of food to eat.

According to *kashrut*, you cannot eat meat and dairy together. Kosher delis serve meat, so they're perfect for a carnivore. At the deli, you can order sandwiches and foods like **chopped liver**, **kasha varnishkes** (bowtie pasta with barley) and **matzoh ball soup** (Soup with dumplings made from ground-up *matzoh*, a kind of hard cracker), **rugalach** (a type of cookie), and even **celery-flavored soda**.

Coney Island Boardwalk

Brooklyn — Coney Island

Since the 1920s, people and dinosaurs from all over New York City have spent their summers on the Coney Island Boardwalk. Visitors may come for the famous amusement parks and brave the Cyclone—an 85-foot tall wooden roller coaster—or they may spend the day eating through the boardwalk's food stalls, featuring an assortment of street food from all over the world.

On the boardwalk, you can find a huge, warm **pretzel** covered in salt, a city staple. You can also find **frozen ices** (from Italy), crispy **knishes** (mashed potatoes covered in fried dough, brought to New York by Jewish people from Eastern Europe), **frog legs** (from France) and **hot dogs**, which may have been invented right here in New York—depending on who you ask.

FIND:

PRETZEL

WHAT ARE FROG LEGS MADE FROM?
ER.., FROGS, WHY?
WAITAMINUTE. WHAT ARE HOT DOGS MADE OF??
DELICATESSEN
Buffet Catering
FRESH CUT FRIES
FRIED CHICKEN FROG LEGS
GYROS AND KEBABS
SODA·WINGS
Cotton Candy
TACOS
SEAFOOD
CLAM BAR
ITALIAN SAUSAGE
COLD DRINKS
HOT DOGS
SPECIALS
SAUSAGE W/ PEPPERS 7—
FRIED SHRIMP 12—

Bosco's Tea House

Queens — Flushing

In Chinese, **dim sum** (點心) may mean something like "heart's delight." It's a special way of eating where bite-sized amounts of food are shared between family, friends, or dinosaurs, accompanied by pots and pots of hot tea. In fact, some just call this "yum cha" (飲茶), which means "drink tea." Cantonese restaurants serve dim sum from wheeled carts covered with baskets of dumplings, or from small plates piled high with hot, delicious food.

If you go for dim sum, catch a cart serving 蝦餃 (hā gáau, or **shrimp dumpling**), 燒賣 (sīu máai, **dumplings with pork and shrimp**), 叉燒包 (chā sīu bāau, **a bun with sweet pork filling**), with 蘿蔔糕 (lòh baahk gōu, or **turnip cake**), and 蛋撻 (dahn tāat, an **egg tart**) for dessert.

FIND:

DO YOU THINK THEY HAVE LONGER CHOPSTICKS?
WE CAN ASK!

USED
RECORDS
ODO
SECURITY, Inc
QUEENS
DENTISTRY
GENKO OLIVE OIL
Imports & Exports
by Al Ketab
HALAL حلال
SHWARMA • FALAFEL • RICE
Combo
w/ RICE
Chicken
Pita
Soda 3.00
Juice ... 3.00

Mo's Halal Truck

Queens — Astoria

Under the elevated train tracks in Queens, you can find food trucks serving delicious halal food, dishes prepared according to Muslim dietary rules. Many halal carts offer **shwarma**, meat cooked on a constantly-turning spit so it's always hot. Shwarma may be served in a **pita** stuffed with lettuce, tomato, and pickles, or on a platter with rice. You can also find **shish kebab**—meat and vegetables on a skewer, cooked over a hot grill.

If you're an herbivore, there's **falafel** (fried balls made from chickpeas and spices), humus (a savory dip, also made from chickpeas), or baba ganoush (a smoky dip made from eggplant). Cover everything with hot sauce and yogurt sauce, or with **tahini**, a sauce made from sesame seeds.

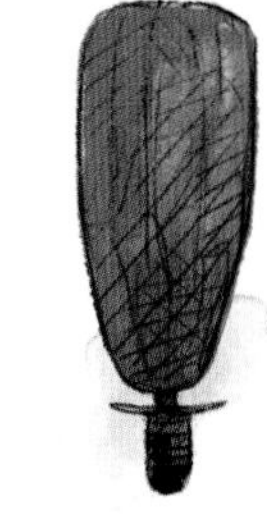

... AND MAKE SURE THE CANNOLIS ARE FRESH.

Brucato's Italian Bakery

Arthur Avenue — The Bronx

In New York, most Italian bakeries specialize in pastries and cookies, or biscotti in Italian. At Italian bakeries, biscotti come in many different shapes, colors, and flavors. Biscotti are sold by the pound, and packaged in **a white box with a red and white string**. They're a perfect gift if you're visiting friends or dinosaurs.

At some cafes and coffee shops, they might only use the word biscotti to mean anisette toast (long, crunchy cookies that taste faintly of licorice and are wonderful dipped in coffee), but in Italian bakeries, biscotti can refer to any cookie or biscuit, including **rainbow cookies** (spongy cookies layered to resemble the Italian flag), and **pignoli** (small, chewy cookies made with almond paste and covered with pine nuts). Bakeries may also serve **cannoli** (fried dough pastries filled with cream), and **espresso** (strong, rich coffee served in tiny cups).

FIND:

Fisch & Daughters Appetizer

Lower East Side — Manhattan

Jewish appetizers are stores that serve food to eat with bagels. You can order your **bagel** toasted, with a *schmear* (Yiddish for cream cheese spread), a *schmear* and lox, which is salmon that has been salted and smoked, or even some **herring**. Your bagel would go good with an **egg cream**, a creamy, frothy drink made by mixing milk, chocolate syrup, and seltzer water. While you're at it, maybe order some **latkes**—fried potato pancakes—which taste amazing with sour cream or applesauce.

If your dinosaur doesn't like bagels, you can order a basket of bialys, baked rolls flavored with chopped onions. Finally, try the **halva**, a candy made from sesame seeds.

"A moltsayt on a tsimes is vi a mayse on a moshl." That's a Yiddish saying that means, "A meal without something sweet is like a story without a moral." The moral of this story is, eat dessert!

KAPCHUNKAS
BIALYS
STURGEON
LOX
SMOKED FISH
5.00
7.00
12.00
EVERYTHING
SALT
PLAIN
PUMPERNICKEL
BAGELS
BIALYS $1
RYE
CHALLAH 6^{99}
Symplectic Geometry

The Famous JOE'S
ORIGINAL
EW YORK
IZZA
BAY ST
RICHMOND AV
PIZZA
MENU
UND SLICE 3.00
LIAN SLICE 3.00
SPUMONI
LLA, CHOC., PISTACIO

Famous Joe's Original New York Pizza

Staten Island

Some say pizza was invented in Italy, some say it was invented in America, but it doesn't really matter, because the best pizza comes from New York.

New Yorkers call their pizzas "pies." Pizza pies are made round or square, and you can order a whole pie or just a **slice** (or three). Round pies have thin crusts and are cut into big, floppy slices; locals eat the slices by folding them in half. The square pies are called Sicilian pizza, and have a thick, chewy crust. New York pizza comes with any toppings you want, except pineapple. Absolutely **no pineapple**, even if you're a dinosaur.

New Yorkers eat pizza with their hands, preferably standing up. If you want extra flavor, you can add parmesan cheese, garlic powder, or **red pepper**. **Spumoni**, a multi-flavored Italian ice cream, is for dessert. Be prepared to use **plenty of napkins**.

EPILOGUE

Staten Island Ferry
I CAN'T BELIEVE YOU DON'T LIKE PIZZA.
I DON'T EVEN WANT TO TALK ABOUT IT.
WELL, OTHER THAN PIZZA, WHAT DID YOU THINK?
WHAT WAS YOUR FAVORITE FOOD?
AHEM.
...YES?

I ATE EVERYTHING YOU WANTED ME TO. YOU OWE ME A CORNED BEEF SANDWICH.
MY CORNED BEEF SANDWICH.
OH... RIGHT.
hmph.
munch!
SO...
FAVORITE FOOD I'VE EATEN TODAY?
YES!!

CORNED BEEF!

the end

AUTHOR'S NOTE

Unlike its predecessor, *Bolivar Eats New York* took less than five years to illustrate. After *Bolivar* was published in 2017, BOOM! Studios and I both knew we wanted to continue exploring the world of Sybil and Bolivar. The prospect of another graphic novel, created on the scale of the first, was daunting. The solution, suggested by my publisher, was a "Discovery Adventure." Immediately, it sounded like the kind of book I wanted to draw.

I am indebted to my editor, Sierra Hahn, for suggesting we take the characters to all five boroughs for this outing, and to my wife, Lucy Guarnera, for realizing the book had to be about food.

Given the sheer size of New York City, and its amazing ethnic and culinary diversity, any book like this would have to assume a somewhat narrow focus or else be hundreds of pages long. In the end, many of the dishes and places chosen include foods that were important to me during my childhood. These foods would be especially familiar to anyone acquainted with the large immigrant communities of southern Italians and Ashkenazi Jews that once thrived in all five boroughs. My family—and our kitchen—make a claim to both communities.

Of course, a number of important foods were not featured. These include, in no particular order, Korean, Soul Food, Dominican, Russian, and Polish cuisine. If Sybil ever convinces Bolivar to join her on another tour, these are some of the first foods they'll try.

The restaurants visited in this book are fictional, but they are composites of several real places. So far as I know, there is no "The Famous Joe's Original New York Pizza;" however, there are several real pizzerias that inspired aspects of Joe's. Not all of them are on Staten Island. Brucato's Italian Bakery, which I located on Arthur Avenue in the Bronx, is partially based on other bakeries that once existed in Brooklyn. In this way, I hope each one of the locations is viewed as a type, and not as secret stand-in for a particular restaurant.

Growing up in Brooklyn meant growing up in a city composed of many smaller ethnic communities, and with many families of first-generation immigrants. Going over to a friend's house, you didn't know if you'd be eating dinner with a fork or chopsticks, or if your friend's family kept special dietary laws you'd be expected to follow. My parents taught me two rules about what to do when I encountered a new kind of food, rules that I carried with me outside of Brooklyn and even into the strange lands of Virginia and South Carolina. We've taught these rules to our sons, too.

First, be thankful and appreciative for whatever you're served.

Second, be sure to try at least one bite of everything in front of you.

Daniel Island
Easter, 2019

ABOUT THE AUTHOR

SEAN RUBIN was born in Brooklyn, New York. As a city kid, he entertained himself by collecting interesting things, learning about obscure subjects, and drawing characters from books. *Bolivar*, the first book Sean both wrote and illustrated, received three starred reviews and was nominated for an Eisner award, an ELG, and a Ringo award. Sean was nominated for the 2018 Russ Manning Award for Most Promising Newcomer, a comics industry honor, for his work on *Bolivar*. Sean's first comics story was a contribution to the Eisner-winning *Mouse Guard: Legends of the Guard* anthology. He is also an illustrator for the *New York Times* Best-selling *Redwall* Series and *The Astronaut Who Painted The Moon*. Sean studied Art and Archeology at Princeton University, where he met his wife, Lucy. They have two sons and live in Charlottesville, Virginia.

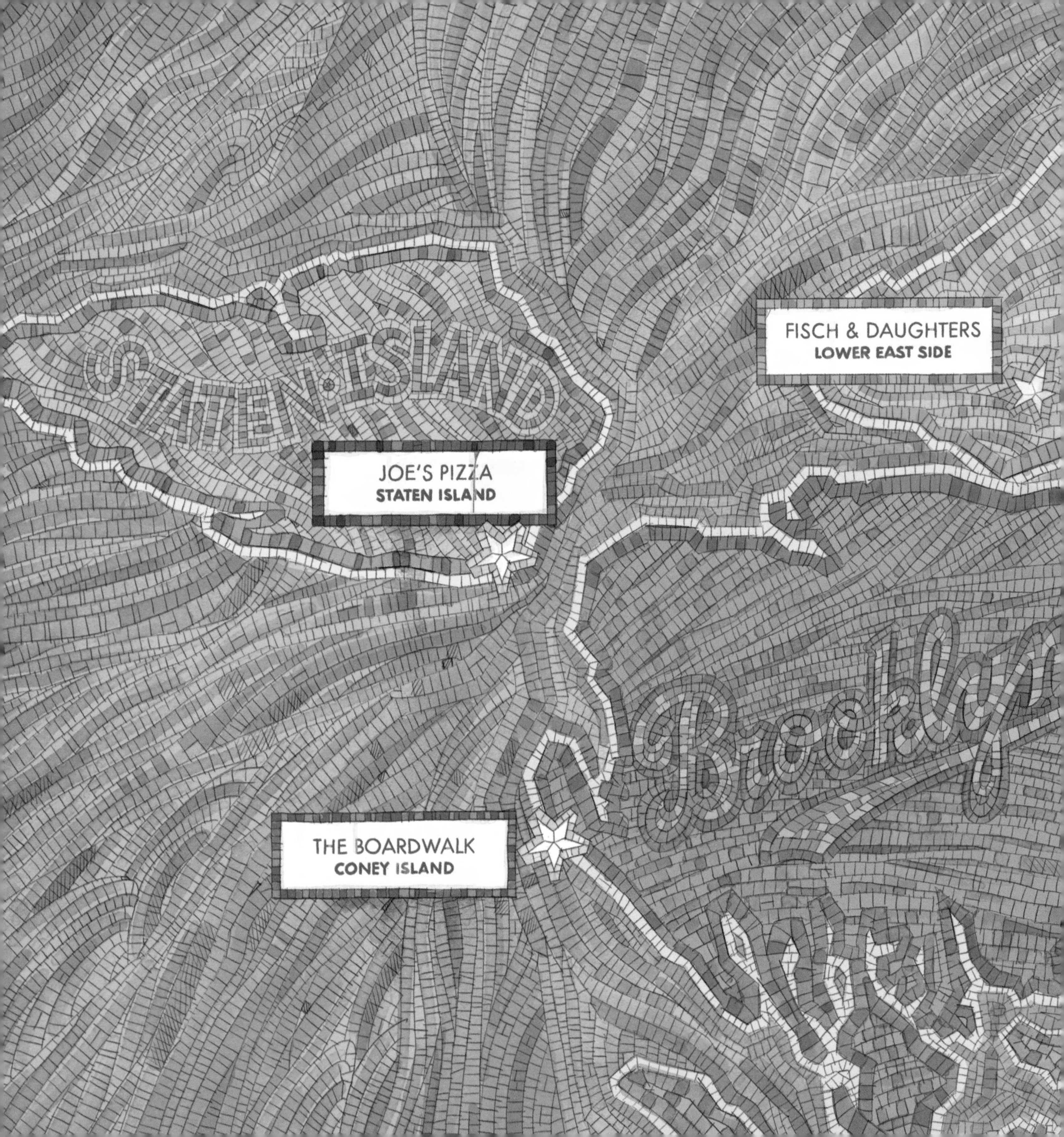
STATEN ISLAND
FISCH & DAUGHTERS
LOWER EAST SIDE
JOE'S PIZZA
STATEN ISLAND
THE BOARDWALK
CONEY ISLAND